THOMAS' SNOWSUIT

Story – Robert Munsch
Art – Michael Martchenko

Annick Press Ltd.
Toronto • New York • Vancouver

©1985 Bob Munsch Enterprises Ltd. (text)
©1985 Michael Martchenko (art)

Twenty-ninth printing, June 1999

Annick Press Ltd.

We acknowledge the support of the Canada Council
for the Arts for our publishing program. We also thank
the Ontario Arts Council.

Cataloguing in Publication Data
  Munsch, Robert N., 1945-
    Thomas' snowsuit

  (Munsch for kids)
  ISBN 0-920303-32-3 (bound).— ISBN 0-920303-33-1 (pbk.)

  I. Martchenko, Michael. II. Title. III. Series:
  Munsch, Robert N., 1945- Munsch for kids

  PS8576.U58T46 1985 jC813'.54 C85-0992540-0
  PZ7.M86Th 1985

Distributed in Canada by: Published in the U.S.A. by Annick Press (U.S.) Ltd.
Firefly Books Ltd.   Distributed in the U.S.A. by:
3680 Victoria Park Avenue   Firefly Books (U.S.) Inc.
Willowdale, ON   P.O. Box 1338
M2H 3K1   Ellicott Station
                                Buffalo, NY 14205

Printed on acid-free paper.

Printed and bound in Canada by Friesens, Altona, Manitoba

To Otis and Erika Wein in Halifax,
who helped me make up this story,
and to Danny Munsch

One day, Thomas' mother bought him a nice new brown snowsuit. When Thomas saw that snowsuit he said, "That is the ugliest thing I have ever seen in my life. If you think that I am going to wear that ugly snowsuit, you are crazy!"

Thomas' mother said, "We will see about that."

The next day, when it was time to go to school, the mother said, "Thomas, please put on your snowsuit," and Thomas said, "NNNNNO."

His mother jumped up and down and said, "Thomas, put on that snowsuit!"

And Thomas said, "NNNNNO!"

So Thomas' mother picked up Thomas in one hand, picked up the snowsuit in the other hand, and she tried to stick them together. They had an enormous fight, and when it was done Thomas was in his snowsuit.

Thomas went off to school and hung up his snowsuit. When it was time to go outside, all the other kids jumped into their snowsuits and ran out the door. But not Thomas.

The teacher looked at Thomas and said, "Thomas, please put on your snowsuit."

Thomas said, "NNNNNO."

The teacher jumped up and down and said, "Thomas, put on that snowsuit."

And Thomas said, "NNNNNO."

So the teacher picked up Thomas in one hand, picked up the snowsuit in the other hand, and she tried to stick them together. They had an enormous fight, and when they were done the teacher was wearing Thomas' snowsuit and Thomas was wearing the teacher's dress.

When the teacher saw what she was wearing, she picked up Thomas in one hand and tried to get him back into his snowsuit. They had an enormous fight. When they were done, the snowsuit and the dress were tied into a great big knot on the floor and Thomas and the teacher were in their underclothes.

Just then the door opened, and in walked the principal. The teacher said, "It's Thomas. He won't put on his snowsuit."

The principal gave his very best
PRINCIPAL LOOK and said, "Thomas, put
on your snowsuit."

And Thomas said, "NNNNNO."

So the principal picked up Thomas in one hand and he picked up the teacher in the other hand, and he tried to get them back into their clothes. When he was done, the principal was wearing the teacher's dress, the teacher was wearing the principal's suit and Thomas was still in his underwear.

Then from far out in the playground someone yelled, "Thomas, come and play!" Thomas ran across the room, jumped into his snowsuit, got his boots on in two seconds and ran out the door.

The principal looked at the teacher and said, "Hey, you have on my suit. Take it off right now."

The teacher said, "Oh, no. You have on my dress. You take off my dress first."

Well, they argued and argued and argued, but neither one wanted to change first.

Finally, Thomas came in from recess. He looked at the principal and he looked at the teacher. Thomas picked up the principal in one hand. He picked up the teacher in the other hand. They had an enormous fight and Thomas got everybody back into their clothes.

The next day the principal quit his job and moved to Arizona, where nobody ever wears a snowsuit.

Other books in the Munsch for Kids series:

The Dark
Mud Puddle
The Paper Bag Princess
The Boy in the Drawer
Jonathan Cleaned Up, Then He Heard a Sound
Murmel Murmel Murmel
Millicent and the Wind
Mortimer
The Fire Station
Angela's Airplane
David's Father
50 Below Zero
I Have to Go!
Moira's Birthday
A Promise is a Promise
Pigs
Something Good
Show and Tell
Purple, Green and Yellow
Wait and See
Where is Gah-Ning?
From Far Away
Stephanie's Ponytail
Munschworks
Munschworks 2

Many Munsch titles are available in French and/or
Spanish. Please contact your favorite supplier.